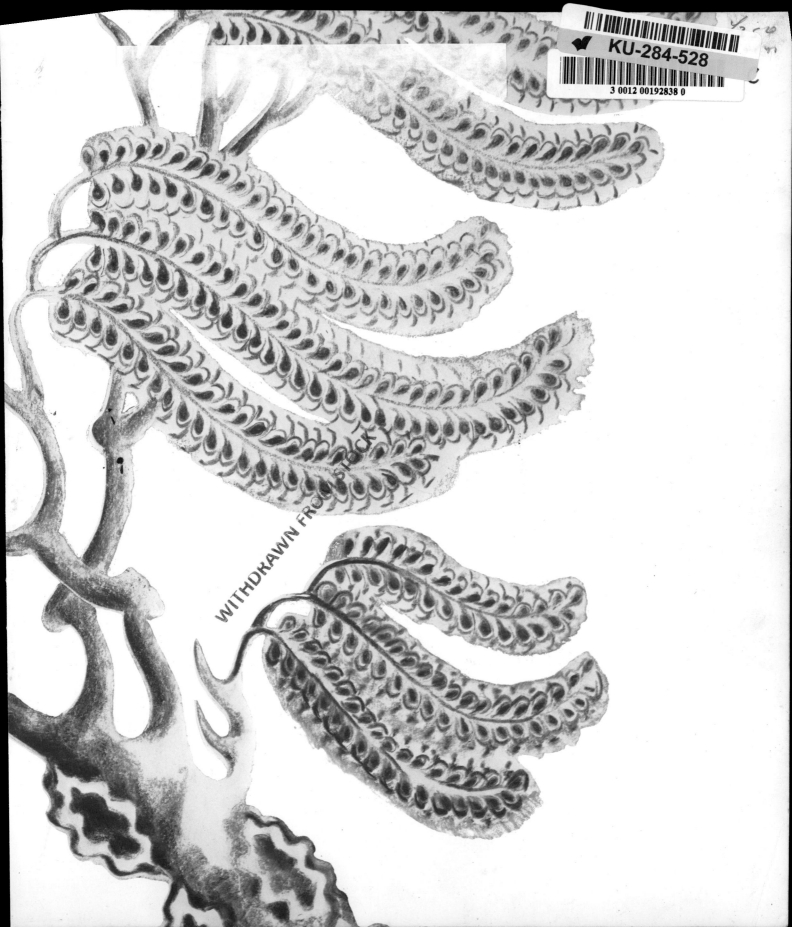

the WILLOW PATTERN STORY

Angus & Robertson Publishers
London • Sydney • Melbourne • Singapore • Manila

First published by Angus & Robertson Publishers, Australia, 1978

© Text Angus & Robertson Publishers 1978
© Illustrations Lucienne Fontannaz 1978

National Library of Australia
Cataloguing-in-publication data.

Fontannaz, Lucienne.
  The willow pattern story.

ISBN 0 207 13848 6

  1. Legends, Chinese. 2. Tales, Chinese.
  I. Title.

398.2′0951

Printed in Hong Kong

the WILLOW PATTERN STORY

Lucienne Fontannaz   *text by* Barbara Ker Wilson

ANGUS & ROBERTSON PUBLISHERS

This is a love story set beneath a weeping-willow tree which once grew beside a swift-flowing river, in the days when China was ruled by Emperors, long ago.

It happened that a rich mandarin, T'so Ling, built a large and splendid house close to that swift-flowing river, and far from the city where he used to work in the service of the Emperor. T'so Ling's wife had died, and he shared his new house with his only daughter, Koong-se, a young woman of great beauty. T'so Ling and Koong-se had servants to wait upon them and possessed everything the heart could desire — except happiness.

T'so Ling was unhappy because in the days when he had served the Emperor, he had accepted bribes from those who wished to gain his favour. Now he was afraid that his bad deeds might be discovered. He had a faithful clerk, a humble young man whose name was Chang. T'so Ling brought Chang to his country house and ordered him to destroy every record of his dishonesty. This work occupied many weeks.

Koong-se was unhappy because she had fallen in love with Chang, the humble clerk and poet. That is to say, she was both unhappy and happy. She was happy because she was able to see Chang every day in her father's house; she was unhappy because she knew that they would never be able to spend their lives together. What! Koong-se, the beautiful daughter of a rich mandarin, marry a humble clerk? The very idea was absurd.

As for Chang, he returned the beautiful Koong-se's love. Each day, when he had finished his work, he would write an exquisite love poem for her. Alas! Soon all the records would be destroyed; his work would be finished. Then he must go away. He would never see Koong-se again.

Now Koong-se had a young handmaid, the wife of the gardener who tended the trees and flowers that grew around the mandarin's splendid house: persimmon and peach and flowering almond trees, camellias, white and pink, purple iris and deep-red peonies. Koong-se's handmaid knew that her mistress and Chang had fallen in love, and she saw how the two lovers sighed because they could not hope to live happily ever afterwards. With her help Koong-se and Chang used to meet secretly each evening in a little summer-house in one corner of the garden, and then Chang would read aloud his latest poem. Sometimes his poems were happy and light-hearted; sometimes they were sad. For such was the love of Koong-se and Chang: happy and light-hearted one moment, sad the next.

One evening, Koong-se unclasped a string of blue beads from her neck and gave them to Chang. "They are not as beautiful as your poems," she told him. "But keep them for my sake."

It happened that T'so Ling walked in his garden to admire the flowers and enjoy their scent upon the night air. He discovered his daughter and Chang in the summer-house and was filled with rage. Immediately he sent Chang away and ordered him never to set foot upon his land again, on pain of death. "As for you," he told Koong-se, "from now on I forbid you to go outside the walls of my house!"

The next day, T'so Ling appointed a new handmaid to serve his daughter, an old woman whose heart was as shrivelled as her face. She had no sympathy for those who loved.

That was not all: fearing that Chang might dare to disobey him, and try to visit his daughter secretly, T'so Ling ordered a high wooden fence to be built around his house. He built on to the house a set of rooms for her, jutting out over the water's edge, with a terrace where she might walk. The only way to enter or leave the rooms where Koong-se was imprisoned was to pass through T'so Ling's great hall, where he spent most of his time. Moreover, the windows of the great hall overlooked the river — there was no chance that Chang might row a boat over to the house. And if he tried to cross the bridge that spanned the river where a weeping-willow grew, he would be seen at once. In this way, T'so Ling ensured that it would be impossible for the two lovers ever to meet again. He was well satisfied with his work.

Soon afterwards, T'so Ling came to give his daughter an important piece of news.

"I have arranged for your betrothal to one of my most respected friends, a Ta-jin of high rank and great wealth," he told Koong-se. "He is the same age as myself, and a widower. You are fortunate indeed to marry a man of such importance. Soon he will come to visit here." T'so Ling looked out of the window, where a peach tree grew against the wall. "You will be married when the peach tree blossoms, in the Spring."

Koong-se was in despair when she heard her father's words. It seemed that there was nothing she could do to avert her fate. She too glanced out of the window and saw that, as yet, the peach tree had scarcely formed its buds. She shuddered to think of the time when it would burst into blossom.

"How lucky you are!" exclaimed the old handmaid, with a toothless smile. "What more could a young girl ask than to obtain a husband who is wise, wealthy and of high rank?"

Koong-se could not answer her; the thoughts in her young heart were as bitter as the kernel of a peach stone. And yet, as the days went by, she was cheered by one happy omen: a bird came and built its nest in the branches of the peach tree. How Koong-se envied that little bird, able to fly back and forth as freely as it pleased!

One afternoon, as Koong-se walked along the terrace beside the swift-flowing river, with the old handmaid following a few steps behind her, she saw one half of a coconut shell floating towards the river bank. Curious, she drew it towards her with her parasol and took it out of the water. Imagine her surprise and joy when she found inside the shell one of the blue beads she had given to Chang, and a message written on a piece of bamboo paper!

"What have you found?" the old handmaid asked suspiciously, hobbling to her side.

"It is nothing," Koong-se answered carelessly, although her heart was beating as fast as a bird's wing. She threw the shell to the ground, but concealed its contents inside her folded parasol.

As soon as Koong-se was alone, she opened the paper and read what Chang had inscribed on it: a poem, and a message.

The poem spoke of the bird's nest in the peach tree by her window, and as she read it Koong-se realized with a start that Chang must somehow be near her — near enough to see the nest hidden in the leafy branches! The message said: *As the shell drifted towards you, so my thoughts speed always in the same direction. But when the peach tree blossoms and my love is taken from me by another, your faithful Chang will sink beneath the deep waters of the river.*

Koong-se was deeply troubled when she read Chang's words, for she understood only too well that he intended to destroy himself once she was married to the Ta-jin. He would prove his constancy by death. It was a message of despair. How could she send him an answer? That night, she took her ivory writing tablet and used her embroidery needle to scratch some words on its smooth surface: *Do not wise farmers gather the fruit they fear will be taken from them? Come and gather the fruit you desire before the peach tree drops its blossom.*

Early the next morning, Koong-se managed to go out alone to the river bank. She found the coconut shell lying where she had thrown it the day before, and placed her ivory tablet inside it. Then she launched it upon the water. The swift current drew it away and it floated off through the morning mist, until she could see it no longer.

Days and weeks went by, and the peach tree buds were about to burst into blossom. But Koong-se received no further message from Chang. Hope flickered low in her heart.

And now a mighty noise and bustle announced the coming of her betrothed, the great lord, the Ta-jin himself! He arrived to take food and wine in T'so Ling's house, according to custom, before the marriage ceremony should take place. The Ta-jin's servants walked before him, beating gongs and shouting out his achievements in war. His many titles were inscribed in vermilion characters on paper lanterns held high above their heads.

Koong-se would not meet her bridegroom face to face until the marriage ceremony itself, but in the meantime her father brought her a large lacquered box filled with precious jewels — a wedding present from the Ta-jin.

"See what splendid gems he has sent you!" T'so Ling exclaimed, but Koong-se glanced at the sparkling jewels without interest. She felt like a bird caught in a net, powerless to escape her fate.

T'so Ling entertained his distinguished guest in the great hall adjoining Koong-se's rooms. The wine flowed freely as they drank to each other and to the forthcoming marriage. They drank so much that presently they began to sing and shout, and Koong-se heard the rattle of a wine cup knocked to the floor. The sounds of revelry could be heard in the dark garden . . . where, in the deep shadow of a cypress tree, a stranger waited silently.

Who was he, this stranger? Presently he entered the porch of the house, where he found a coat discarded by one of T'so Ling's servants. There was no one about to challenge him — for the servants of both T'so Ling and the Ta-jin were copying their masters' example, and drinking the night away in their own quarters.

The stranger put on the coat and, disguised as one of the household, crossed the great hall unnoticed by either T'so Ling or his drunken guest. In another moment he had entered Koong-se's apartment: in truth this was no stranger, but Chang, who had come at last to take Koong-se away with him.

Joyfully the lovers embraced, and spoke to each other softly, lest they should rouse the old handmaid, whose snores reverberated through the screen that divided her sleeping-room from Koong-se's apartment.

"Come!" Chang whispered. "The peach blossom droops upon the bough. We must fly from here tonight!"

Koong-se gave Chang the lacquered box of jewels. Then she took up her distaff, still with a bunch of flax wound round it, and together the lovers tiptoed through the great hall, where now T'so Ling and the Ta-jin nodded sleepily over their wine cups. They fled into the garden, and ran towards the bridge where the graceful weeping-willow stood.

Just as they neared the bridge, T'so Ling stirred in his drunken slumber. He glanced into the garden and glimpsed a fleeing figure, his daughter! With a great cry of rage he picked up a long hunting whip that lay to hand, and staggered out to pursue Koong-se and Chang. But the old mandarin could not hope to overtake the young lovers. A little way across the bridge, on the farther bank of the river, he gave up the pursuit and returned to his house. Here he found that the Ta-jin, learning what had happened, had fallen into a furious passion. It took the combined efforts of all his servants (many of whom were as drunk as their lord) to calm him down. And so Koong-se and Chang made good their escape.

In the days that followed, as the peach blossom fell from the bough and lay scattered on the ground like fallen snow, T'so Ling and the Ta-jin made every effort to discover the whereabouts of Koong-se and Chang. They sent their servants throughout the countryside to seek them; but evening after evening the servants returned without any news. Gradually T'so Ling fell into the ill-humour of despair, but the Ta-jin swore a terrible vow of vengeance against Chang. He knew as a magistrate that he could have Chang put to death because he had taken the jewels he gave Koong-se. As for Koong-se herself, he decreed that she should also die unless she fulfilled her father's wishes and returned to become his bride.

Had the old mandarin and the Ta-jin but known it, the lovers were in fact hidden at no great distance from T'so Ling's house, in a simple dwelling overlooking the river not far from the bridge. Here T'so Ling's gardener lived with his wife — the young handmaid who had been dismissed from Koong-se's service when T'so Ling first learned of the secret meetings between Chang and his daughter.

In this little house Koong-se and Chang were married with simple ceremony, and here they continued to live in close concealment, venturing out only after nightfall. The gardener kept them informed of the Ta-jin's continuing efforts to find them. They made a plan that if on any day the gardener did not return home from work at his usual hour, that would be a sign that suspicion had fallen on the house.

One day, T'so Ling sent soldiers about the countryside to proclaim that if his daughter were to forsake Chang and return home she would be forgiven. But if Chang were found he would be executed. Although it was still daylight, Chang left the little house and went down into the village street to hear the proclamation. He rejoiced to think that T'so Ling could relent so far as to offer his daughter forgiveness, even though he knew that Koong-se would never consent to return to him. As he stood in the street there were those who asked each other who he was, and whispered among themselves.

That evening the gardener did not return home at his usual hour, and then Koong-se trembled, for she knew that suspicion had fallen upon the house. A little later a soldier came to the door. He demanded to know from the gardener's wife whether she was hiding the two lovers.

"A great reward is offered to anyone who helps to restore Chang and Koong-se to justice," the soldier said. "If they are hidden here there is no way they may escape. I have set a guard in the street, and the river flows behind the house."

The gardener's wife was determined not to betray the lovers. She decided to keep the soldiers talking so that Koong-se and Chang, hidden in their room, might have time to work out some plan.

"I think I know where Chang may be hiding," she said in a loud voice, so that Koong-se and Chang might hear her words. "I believe he is in a house not far from here. But before I tell you, I must have the definite promise of the reward, in a letter signed by the mandarin himself."

"Very well," said the soldier, "I will go straight away to get the letter. But I will leave a guard posted at your door, just in case you are deceiving me."

As soon as he had gone the gardener's wife went into the other room. "We must devise some plan!" she said. "You cannot escape past the guard at the street door." She looked out of the open window. "There is only one way," she told Chang, "the river is your one chance of escape."

Koong-se cried aloud as she looked down on the rushing waters, swollen now by early rains.

"Yes, it is my only chance," Chang said. "Better to drown in the flood than be butchered by the soldiers." He turned to Koong-se. "Be brave and trust me," he said. "Somehow I will swim across the river and return for you in a boat."

Then he went over to the window and leapt into the river below. Koong-se hung out of the window, watching his fearful struggle in the roaring waters. She saw him gain the middle of the torrent, then the rapid current carried him from sight. There was nothing she could do save stay hidden and wait for his return . . . if he had not drowned.

Time passed. Suddenly there was a loud knocking at the door. The gardener's wife opened it. The soldier had returned with a letter from the mandarin. It promised a large sum of money to anyone who would deliver up Chang and restore Koong-se to her father. Still trying to cause as long a delay as possible, the woman told the soldier that it was useless to try to find Chang until moonrise, when he often walked in a nearby rice field. There it would be easy to capture him. Meanwhile, she gave the soldier some rice wine and managed to while away a full hour. At one point, the soldier went out to speak to the guard at the door, and then the gardener's wife quickly slipped into the other room.

Koong-se had gone! There were wet footmarks and dripping garments on the floor. The footmarks led to the window. The gardener's wife glanced outside: a boat had just pushed off from shore. She had no doubt that brave Chang and her beloved mistress, Koong-se, were in it. Hastily she removed all traces of the flight from the room, then returned to the soldier. By now the moon had risen, and she lit a lamp.

"I can delay no longer!" the soldier said. "I still cannot be sure that you are not deceiving me, woman!" He ordered the guard to search the house, but he found no one and nothing of value. The precious jewels which the Ta-jin had given Koong-se were now in the boat on the river, with the lovers.

"Very well," growled the soldier, "now we will go to the rice field."

They did so, walking by the light of the moon. But, needless to say, Chang was not there.

Angry at having wasted so much time, the soldier left and the woman went back to her house, to find that her husband had now returned. She told him everything that had happened, and he praised her cleverness.

Meanwhile, the boat bearing Koong-se and Chang made its way down the swift-flowing river through the night. When dawn came, they were near the entrance to the great Yangtse-kian river. Chang needed all his skill to steer the boat safely into its wide waters. The Yangtse-kian was thronged with craft; they were amongst a fleet of boats that had taken the yearly tribute of salt and rice westward to the court of the Emperor, and were now returning home.

For several days they sailed towards the sea. Chang knew that before long they must reach a river station where all outgoing boats were examined by officials. This they must avoid at all costs. One morning, they reached a small island in the river, and here Chang moored the boat.

It was a pleasant little island, quite uninhabited. "Let us make this our home," Chang said to Koong-se.

"Oh yes!" she said, looking about her in delight. "We will spend the rest of our days here in peace and happiness!"

Chang sold the Ta-jin's jewels in the towns nearby, and with the proceeds he was able to buy the right to live on the island, besides all the necessities of life. Together, Chang and Koong-se built a small house and tilled the land, sowing seed and planting trees.

Years went by. Their crops prospered, their trees bore fruit. Sons were born to Chang and Koong-se; happy children who laughed and sang and did not know anger, or fear, or despair. Chang returned to his literary pursuits, and besides his poems he wrote a book on agriculture which gained him a great reputation in that distant province where the island lay, — and even beyond it.

But it was this that in the end brought tragedy to Chang and Koong-se. For the reputation Chang gained revealed, at last, his whereabouts to the Ta-jin. He was by now a very old man, but his passion for revenge remained unabated.

It did not take long for the Ta-jin to gather an escort of soldiers and attack the little island where Chang and Koong-se had lived in peace and happiness for so long. Luckily their sons were not on the island; they had been sent to the mainland, to live and study at the house of a great scholar.

Chang and Koong-se were quite unprepared for the Ta-jin's attack. The first soldier who leapt on to the island ran Chang through the body with his sword, and he fell dying to the ground.

Koong-se, who had watched the brutal attack in unspeakable horror, ran into the house in sorrow and despair. She set it on fire. Soon the flimsy dwelling was a mass of flames, and she perished in the midst of them.

The Ta-jin had triumphed — or so it seemed. But that was not quite the end of the love story of Chang and Koong-se. For the gods above looked down and cursed the Ta-jin for his cruelty. He died soon afterwards, friendless and unpitied. No children scattered scented paper over his grave. No one mourned his passing.

But the gods rewarded the constancy of Chang and Koong-se by transforming their spirits into two immortal doves. So they fly for ever above the weeping-willow tree, free and perfect in their undying love.

Envoy

Now that the story is ended, one can see that the willow pattern illustrates each part of the love story of Koong-se and Chang. It shows the splendid house built by the mandarin T'so Ling; the high wall and the apartments overlooking the swift-flowing river which he added after Chang's banishment; the bridge, overhung by a weeping-willow, that led across the river, on which T'so Ling with his hunting whip is pursuing Koong-se, bearing her distaff, and Chang carrying the Ta-jin's jewels; the gardener's house where the lovers hid, the boat in which they escaped, and the little island with the dwelling that Koong-se set on fire after Chang was killed. Finally, it shows the two immortal doves, symbols of constancy and undying love.